AUTHOR OF THE BESTSELLING
More than Words

A Strange & Wicked Magic

POETRY & SHORT STORIES

ZACK SHAH

A STRANGE & WICKED MAGIC

The fell types are digitally reproduced by Igino Marini.
www.iginomarini.com
Books may be purchased by contacting the publisher and author at:
penwingspublishing@gmail.com
Author: Zack Shah
Cover Design: Iffah Hazirah
Publisher: Penwings Publishing
Editor: Penwings Publishing
ISBN: 978-967-14227-7-9
1. Poetry 2. Fiction
First Edition

Printed by:
Percetakan Okid Sdn Bhd
No. 2, Jalan SS 13/3C, Subang Jaya Industrial Estate,
47500, Subang Jaya, Selangor, Malaysia.

Published by: Penwings Publishing
Subang Jaya, Selangor Darul Ehsan, Malaysia.

CONTENTS

Lost Souls

- CHAPTER I -
Fallen Stars

- CHAPTER II -
City of Sadness

- CHAPTER III -

Always and Forever

Déjà vu

Incantations

Twisted Tales

Foreword

For smitten hearts
        and lovelorn souls,
        for trying times
        in joy and grief

For the missing parts
        that once was whole,
        may these rhymes
        bring sweet relief.

Lost Souls

- Chapter I -

Fallen Stars

Parts of You

Your breath, my air
    your shadow, my light
    your tear, my sea.

Your blood in my heart
    your kiss on my soul,
    every part of you in me.

Pieces of Me

Break me, baby,
        I'll let you shatter me
        into a million tiny pieces
        until there's no trace of me left
        but shards on the floor.

Only if you promise,
        to put me back together
        and make me whole once more.

Fallen Stars

She was a galaxy
        in his universe,
        and he was the twinkle
        in her eyes.

They were both fallen stars
        just out of reach,
        in the darkness
        of each other's skies.

Afterglow

The sparks we tend to soaring highs,
        burning, building, writhing slow.

His lips between my aching thighs,
        the parts of him I yearn to know.

The smoke and ember in my sighs,
        I bask within his afterglow.

Bad Decisions

Why does the very sight of you
invoke such primal forces within me
that it's almost impossible to resist
the urge to misbehave?

How am I supposed to say no
when it's the very sight of you I crave?

Stranger Danger

That sexy stubble
on your chin,
the smell of trouble
on your skin.

The pheromones
that you exude
that put my body
in the mood.

That smile between your teeth
that makes my brain go numb;
an omen of more
mischievous things to come.

Cookie Jar

My itchy fingers can't resist
to take a dive despite the risk,
the lovely treats within my fist.
I know by now I must desist,
but just this once my dear,
despite the fate I say I fear,
I simply must insist.

Breadcrumbs

He leaves a trail for me to find,
of promises scattered, in a line.
But I would rather wait
for my hook and bait
to lure him back
and make him mine.

Heaven and Hell

Loving you is
a bittersweet
experience.

A little slice
of heaven,
a little taste
of hell.

A feeling I know,
all too well.

Perfect Storm

We were wind and lightning,
        thunder and rain,
        fire and flood.

Two acts of God raising hell,
        trapped in prisons
        of flesh and blood.

Open to Suggestion

I'm curled up by the fire,
with a glass of wine.

A good book in my hand
ready to unwind.

But I will leave my
late night plans behind,

If you have better things
in mind.

Close Quarters

Nose to nose, face to face
    legs entwined,
    my hand on your chest
    your fingers running through my hair,

Our lips so close they might just touch,
    static building in the air.

Cheek to cheek, brow to brow,
    let's close the space
    between us now.

Medicine

These dreams of you
that haunt my nights,
a painful dose of pure delight.

These ghosts of you
inside my head,
a cruel cure that keeps me fed.

These thoughts of you
that fill my mind,
a bittersweet anodyne.

An Acquired Taste

The honey in her mouth
 the venom on her tongue,

I'd do anything to get a sip
 of those bittersweet lips,

Even if I have to plea
 on bended knee,

For her to let me lick
 those sugarcoated fingertips.

Wallflower

The way you steal the limelight and shine it on me makes me a little anxious, when I'm comfortable just standing in your shadow, shrinking in a corner, invisible, like a flower on a wall.

But you asked me for a dance, despite my objections, told me that I was the belle of the ball. You made me feel like I was special, when I was nothing much at all.

Topsy-Turvy

For you my dear, I'd get high,
    if only to know how it feels
    to be head over heels,
    with my feet in the sky.

Chain Reaction

A spark is all you need
    to set fire to my ocean,
    for I am a storm,
    in human form.

So be careful what you set in motion.

A Chance

You used to sing me poetry
by the side of the street-
now all your poems are broken,
premature and heartbreakingly
incomplete.

Tell me, dear, how can I help
fill your uninspired lips with song
when you've never given me
the chance all along?

Mind Reader

How can you read my mind,
taste my thoughts,
drink my dreams,
and not know the torment
of my desire?

How can you make a meal
out of my memories
and tell me that you don't remember
the feel of the flames,
when you've clearly played
with my fire.

Uncharted Waters

You think you've scoured my ocean floor,
plumbed its intricate world,
met the terrifying and wonderful parts of me
that slumber in the deep.

You say you know what makes me smile,
but do you know what makes me weep?
The dreams I dream when I'm not asleep?

Perfection

I am not just something to look at,
    a pretty thing that you expect
    to stay pretty forever.

I am not an immortal flower
    in a garden of perpetual spring,

I cannot be
    your everything.

Disappointment

How bitter I was when I discovered
        that I was not one of the many
        precious things you'd look for
        to cherish and adore and call your own.

You're with him,
        and I'm alone.

Sacred

My body is a temple,
and I will not defile
what is sacred enough
to come out
of the womb of the divine,
but not holy enough
to please
your earthly desires,
just so I can be
a little less lonely.

NECTAR

You asked me what made me wet. And I answered, with blood, sweat and tears.

I told you, that I am not made of honey and happiness, like all the other souls you look for.

Yet you still stayed for the nectar that would not come for you.

Blurred Lines

This silly game
we sometimes play,
where all we do
is fight all day-

It's a daunting task,
I must confess,
when go means stay
and no means yes,

I do implore,
don't make me guess,
don't ask for more
if you want less.

Liars

He told her that he loved her,
she said she loved him too.
But one of them is lying,
and you're probably wondering who.

Losing Battle

We went to war with weapons drawn
 through rapid waves
 and scorching flame,

With me as your
 unknowing pawn,
 a victim of this cruel game.

We fought with fate
 from dusk till dawn
 and left to tend these wounds of shame.

I looked for you, but you were gone,
 and I was left
 to bear the blame.

Spilt Milk

I teach myself to not be too sentimental, to not lose sleep over broken teacups, to let lost things stay lost. These days when I spill milk, I just wipe up the mess. Just like I did with all the tears I cried, the day I found you on our bed with someone else.

Firestarter

My arms are not for you to hold,
a furnace burns within my soul.

My hands are not for you to take,
you cannot bear the heat they make.

The sparks I breathe lay worlds to waste,
my mouth is not for you to taste.

My dear, can't you not see,
the flame that runs all over me?

Give and Take

This push and pull
that makes no sense,
a tug of war
that never ends,

With you and me
now, at a lost,
past battle lines
that can't be crossed.

Though you may think
that it's unwise,
to settle on
a compromise,

I ask that we
make amends
and give this tale
its proper end

With one last kiss
through tear-filled eyes,
as we exchange
our last goodbyes.

Wake-up Call

The morning sun
as roosters sing,
and all the omens
it may bring,

How can I
remain in bed,
when all the thoughts
inside my head,

Are of things that will
be put at stake,
if I decide
to never wake,

Should I break the bell
before it screams?
or will I let it
end my dreams

Rude Awakening

You were the most beautiful thing I'd ever seen. Glory and grace incarnate. Divinity in human form. Perfection made flesh.

My loved ones told me that you were not what you seemed, but I was deaf to their warnings, blind to the truth.

I couldn't see that you were but a wolf in sheep's clothing, that you were hiding a monster beneath that human flesh, until it was too late.

How could I still be surprised on the day you finally showed your true face, your fangs, your talons, the malice that you have concealed so well?

You tore through my chest with your bare hands, as if my skin was made of paper, ripped my heart out through my rib-cage, and made me watch, as you devoured it whole.

Same Difference

You mistook vodka for water all the time, and wonder why you're always parched and intoxicated. Being with me kept you sated, but I don't make you drunk enough to forget your sadness. You needed the liquor to burn away the sorrow.

You're with him again tonight, but I don't mind. I know I'm not your cup of wine, but don't expect me to be here for you tomorrow.

Shadows

I tried my best to forget you. Like a scar that won't fade, you stayed in my mind, a mark I can't erase. I wish I could touch you one last time, just to see if you were there, if you were ever real at all.

But I am here losing my mind, and you're just a shadow on the wall.

ZACK SHAH

The Missing of You

It's another day without you. Another twenty-four hours without the sunshine of your smile to dispel the darkness in my mind, without your arms to keep me from disintegrating into a thousand, indiscernible pieces, without the heavenly chords of your voice to quiet the demons that haunt me in my dreams. I lay in bed, wishing for sleep that never came, wondering if the missing of you will ever leave my body like how blood leaves a wound. I fear I may be imprisoned in this perpetual night, the empty space next to me a painful reminder of your absence, my skin an immortal desert that will forever thirst for the oasis of your touch.

The silence in this grieving home echoes endlessly like the final song of a dying heart, and the well inside me shatters once more as the memories come flooding like a storm that doesn't stop. I inhale the waters of this deep and desperate sorrow, wanting nothing more than to drown in my own despair. But just as I thought the sadness would strangle and suffocate me, the tears subside like waves at low tide, granting me an unwanted mercy, an unwelcome pardon from the release that I've been wishing for since the day you told me you didn't love me anymore. I think the fatigue of wrestling with the restless regrets of my past must have overwhelmed the fragile pile of flesh and bones that I've become, for I was suddenly overtaken by a comforting blackness that swallows me whole, cold and gentle, like the sweet embrace of Death himself.

It's the next day, and the missing of you never stopped. I don't think it ever will, but it's just one of those things one learns to live with, like a missing limb, or an inoperable benign tumor. But it's lunchtime and my friends are telling their own sad stories and I listen and offer a shoulder to cry on, giving advice when prompted, pretending like I care, wishing I could. But that's what people are for; they distract you from the giant bruise that your heart has become, because when you're all alone, when the memories and moments return, you have no one else to hold on to but yourself.

Now and Then

Our passion used
to shine like gold,
how had we
grown gray and cold.

Your lust for me
was flaming red,
I could not see
that it was dead.

My love for you
had once burned bright,
until your heart
turned black as night,

Although we ended
long ago,
I would give
the world to know.

A Gentle Reminder

Love should be the end-all-be-all of our existence, but the world isn't that kind. Why shouldn't you brave through the doom and gloom, with nothing but the clothes on your back and empty wallets, so long as the love of your life is by your side?

What's the point of this material life anyway? All the money we make, all the ladders we climb, and all the titles we collect, and all the houses we buy. If there is no one who can love us unconditionally, and not for those ephemeral things we own?

Love should keep you warm at night. There's a certain poetry to it, believe me, I know, but reality doesn't always live up to our expectations. And oftentimes, a blanket and a home is more practical.

Yes, he loves you, and you're his Earth and Sun, you breathe through the same lungs, share the same heart, the same soul. But just remember that's not always enough.

Brief Respite

He exorcized the demons from my dreams
        with the fairy dust on his lips
        and calmed my stormy mind
        with his sunshine smile,

If only for a little while.

His arms kept the nightmares
        and monsters
        and goblins at bay,

If only he'd been here to stay.

Sugarcoated

Every time I feel bile
creeping from the back
of my throat
at the mere mention
of your name,

I relieve myself
with the honey
of my words
and take a spoonful
of poetry,

So that I can
swallow you back down
right where you belong
with the rest of my
sugarcoated
memories.

Last Sunset

Jason looked at the sunset. For real, this time.

No curious sideway glances or accidental glimpses at the heavens. But a profound and breathtaking admiration of the impossible. A ball of fire slowly drowning in an ocean of blue.

He wondered what it would look like once he himself reached the final moment of his twilight years. The culmination of an entire human existence. The Big Full Stop to his epic life story.

Would he even get the chance to see his last sunset, his eyes following the path of the light as it gradually disappears from the horizon? Would his soul remember this lifetime as it passed on to the next? Would he get to spend those last seconds with the love of his life?

He gazed at the misshapen clouds as if to divine the omens of his future, and came to the conclusion that perhaps it was okay to never find true love. People make such a big deal out of it.

What was so great about finding your "other half" anyway? As if you were somehow incomplete, or had a part of yourself missing?

Humans are such silly little creatures.

They constantly want things they can't have and spend years of their lives chasing them only to immediately lose interest the moment they get what they want.

Love was just one of the many foolish pursuits mortals enjoy tormenting themselves over.

Up till that point he had been completely happy with the way things were: cheap wine, tears and broken hearts. A string of part-time lovers and failed romances that made his life just interesting enough to be bearable.

He wondered if all his attempts at finding The One were really just about finding himself; to restore the divine, neglected parts buried deep within so that he can finally understand that the only person he should learn to love unconditionally was himself.

But he realized, that that day was far ahead of him, a dream paved with more tears and more broken hearts.

Jason wondered if the Buddha ever found his true love in his path towards enlightenment, and if he had to give it up so that he could achieve eternal peace.

That must have been hard.

"What are we all after, really?" He asked, to no one in particular, his brain trying to stitch together a narrative that would best placate the angry swarm of thoughts in his mind. Alone or not, everyone was just as miserable as he was.

They were all just too proud or too ignorant to admit it, even to themselves.

"I don't need anyone," Jason thought to himself, as he looked at the sunset as it slowly faded from view, its last rays engulfed by the coming night, a flicker of hope beneath a blanket of darkness. It was honestly how he was feeling. Was this what they called a dark night of the soul?

"I'm completely happy on my own," he said, wishing that, at least for a moment, he didn't have to be. After all, how many more sunsets could he enjoy before it was too late to share it with someone he truly cared about other than himself?

Birds of a Feather

There was a time when me and you,
used to share a common hue,
when both our skies were bright as blue
through cotton clouds where we once flew.

Now I am left without a clue
of someone I once thought I knew,

There was a time, if it was true,
when the one that was the most like me
was you.

Cautionary Tale

I remember the story about a girl
who once gave her heart so recklessly
to a boy she thought would keep
it safe for her his whole life through,

Alas, that was not her fate,
she did not have to wait.
He gave it back with no remorse,
neatly torn in chunks of two.

Illusion

Love is the most
beautiful illusion.
A false hope,
a hopeless dream.

It is chaos, cruelty,
and confusion,
served with a side
of peaches and cream.

Something More

Growing up and growing old,
        doing what we're told.

Broken hearts and hopeless dreams,
        good intentions, wicked schemes.

Wedding bells, and true love's kiss,
        there must be more to life than this.

- Chapter II -

City of Sadness

Lost Souls

She looks for bliss in alleyways,
        in mouths that fill her throat with sighs.

To find a home in strangers' arms,
        and lose herself within their eyes.

This restless urge, from deep within,
        to fall in love before she dies.

How sad it is indeed to see,
        how hungry hearts will feast on lies.

Hard Liquor

Strong and bitter
    frost and flame,
    these words describe you
    best of all.

Should your lips
    still taste the same,
    if nothing else
    I can recall.

I must confess-
    just saying your name
    burns my throat
    like alcohol.

Get in Line

I am numb to your betrayals;
to the bruises
that you left on my heart,
and the cruel words
that you have spoken.

For the cracks I bear,
are beyond repair,
and you cannot break
what has been broken.

Until You're Mine

To want you is to never have you,
        within my reach and yet so far.

To touch you is to dream about you,
        wishes on a falling star.

To love you is to hate you,
        a new wound on an old scar.

Don't believe me when I say I'm fine,
        I'll never be, until you're mine.

No One Else

Late nights spending overthinking, staying up wondering if there was anything I'd want more than you, and failing to find an answer.

I'll drink till the bottle is empty and smoke my lungs black. I'll never love another soul, if it means you'll never love me back.

Withdrawal

Give me all the powders,
give me all the pills,
indulge me with all
the cheap distractions
and all the senseless thrills,

But never tell me that
remembering him
is my remedy,
when it's the very thought
of him that kills.

PRIMROSE PATH

Pray away your demons;
    put them to sleep
    feed all the monsters
    that writhe beneath your skin
    with rank incense,
    bitter nectars
    and poppy flowers,

If only to soothe the beast
    that lurks within,
    and while away
    your darkest hours.

Lala Land

Don't ask me what my sadness does
to keep me awake at night,
or what I'll do when life eventually
catches up with me.

I'll figure out how to deal with
my demons somehow,
But I'm content with dreaming
my entire life away for now.

Blue Blood

The gold in her heart,
        the diamonds in her eyes,
        the silver in her tears.

A crown made of flowers,
        a castle made of sand,
        built against her fears.

She sleeps inside
        her kingdom of sorrow,
        she dreams away her years.

Comfort Zone

This bed of roses where I lie
        with thorns that reach up to the sky
        is my little slice of heaven in hell.

Do not tell me I must change
        in a world that is too strange
        when I would rather dwell-

In a poppy field that blooms all year,
        where rainbows never disappear,
        curled up safely in my shell.

So hear my plea,
        leave me be,
        forever in this magic spell.

Desperate Measures

I tried my best to cut you out, to bleed you out from my wounds, to exorcise the ghosts of your memories with holy rituals, to peel off your kisses where they burned through my bones. Anything to get rid of the scent you left on my skin.

But you're still there, inside my veins. Nothing else remains.

Insomnia

What I would do
    to kill the sadness outright,
    just so I can get
    through the night.

But my lonely heart
    is split in two,
    and my head is filled
    with thoughts of you.

Toxic

The scent of you that lingers,
the cigarette smoke of your breath.
I would suck the poison from your fingers,
even if it means my death.

Last Resort

Bury me in all the ashes,
drown me in all the wine.
Let me smoke and drink myself into
the earliest grave I can find.

I'd rather the drugs kill me in the end,
than have you come
and break my heart again.

Ebb and Flow

The sadness comes,
the sadness goes,
I smile, I laugh,
but no one knows.

The waves go by,
without a care,
as I drown
in my despair,

But the water recedes
and I swim to shore,
until the tide comes in
once more.

The sadness shrinks,
the sadness grows,
but that's just how
my ocean flows.

Ocean

You can't drown me,
        my dear,
        I have an ocean of tears
        in my soul.

Do not peer into my eyes,
        darling,
        my sadness can swallow
        you whole.

Sad Girl

Sadness in her soul,
madness in her mind.
She weeps for the love,
she knows she'll never find.

Lost Boy

There is a place I often go
        that no one knows exist,

A realm of untold magic
        that lies beyond the mist,

I fly there when I am sleeping
        or when I'm feeling blue,

Sometimes I come back weeping,
        sometimes I never do.

Once Broken

They tell me that
all wounds will heal,
even the ones
that aren't real.

I don't know what self-help
bull they're reading,
'cause it's been years
and I'm still bleeding.

Will I heal with time
and get better,
or will I stay
this way forever?

Wonder Worker

Beware the witch in her disguise,
do not look into her eyes.

She'll soothe you where it hurts too much,
she'll heal your wounds with just a touch,

The heart they broke she'll mend anew
with words of love and magic glue,

She'll thaw your soul of snow and ice,
if only for a costly price

Beware the witch's magic spells-
you can't afford the help she sells.

Flavors

Love has been a series
of disappointing what-ifs,
of swallowing bitter pills
with sweet nothings
and expecting to
experience a rollercoaster ride
of flavors,
only to find the same
sour aftertaste
on the back of your tongue.

Hopeless Romantic

You say you believe in love at first sight,
I'm sorry if I sound impolite,
but there really is no such thing.

You believe that good always prevails,
like it always does in fairy tales,
and in all the storybooks to which you cling,

You can't expect your happy ending to be
a prince to come on bended knee,
and offer you a wedding ring,

When love does not conquer all
or be there to break your fall
or help you mend your broken wing.

Another Year

A year has passed
for me this day,
so forgive me if I have cause to rue-

I have a rather
pessimistic
point of view.

So keep all your gifts
and good tidings
and all the wishes that don't come true.

Because for me
this birthday hour,
a good night's sleep will do.

Ties that Bind

We tell ourselves that we are free
with our ankles chained to boulders,
when we are all but earthbound souls
with the world upon our shoulders.

City of Sadness

Sidewalks lined with tramps and trash,
        murder and mayhem and cigarette ash.

Shady characters and strangers with sweets,
        wicked souls in one way streets.

Silent moans and muffled screams,
        in alleys paved with broken dreams.

A promised land where dreams come true,
        so long as you pay the devil his due.

Empty Vessels

Hollow hearts
and vacant minds,
finding solace,
blurring lines.

We fill the void
on listless nights,
with smoke and wine
and brief delights.

Seeking safety
where there is none,
from all the things
we can't outrun,

Bloodshot eyes,
lips of blue,
empty hearts
need comfort too.

Fragments

Forgive me
if I am unable
to rearrange
my broken pieces
to fit into
your idea
of what beauty is.

Deception

The quest for acceptance
has led me down
a dark path of deception,
of telling myself
over and over again
that I am enough.

So what's the truth,
my love for my
imperfections
or my desire
to escape them?

Purpose

If it's not my destiny
    to work until my dying day,
    then why am I wasting
    all my precious time away?

If it's not my purpose
    on this earth to pay bills and die,
    then tell me, what the hell
    am I doing here and why?

Monday Blues

Wake me not for life's a chore,
mornings can be such a bore,
so cease your knocking on my door,
I have no care for what's in store.
If you do not wish to see me weeping,
then let me go on sleeping,
for I am weary to the core.

Stories

I enjoy telling stories. Maybe because they offer a glimpse into a world of what-ifs. A universe of possibilities that one could never experience in a bitter reality where the laws of physics are just too harsh and unforgiving. Where magic only exists in children's books. Where happy-ever-afters are only bestowed to the beautiful. Where sadness doesn't just disappear with the wave of a magic wand.

I hide in my stories, in the tales I tell to myself to sleep better at night, or the ones I silently repeat to convince myself that things aren't nearly as bad as they are. You may have similar stories, stories that help you cope with the madness and the misery. These are stories of survival, pretty lies that make life just a little bit more bearable than it actually is. My favorite story is the one where I finally find my soulmate, where we both ride off into the sunset, not a single worry in mind. Where the world itself isn't plotting to punish us for our love.

Wouldn't it be wonderful, to have a prince rescue you from a fearsome dragon, or a fairy godmother to make all your wishes come true? But even fairy tales have their bitter endings; the parts they never tell you about after the book ends. The unwritten chapters, the untold continuation, the unhappy sequels, the not-so-happy-ever-after. How the prince falls out of love with the princess and casts her out of his castle, how the fairy godmother's gifts come with a deadly price that cannot so easily be paid.

I choose to believe that my tale doesn't end in tragedy and terror, but this world we live in isn't so merciful. And the author of my story has been known to be quite clumsy and capricious with his composition, and I fear what terrible plot twists he has in store for me down the line.

Poet's Curse

The impulse to write,
will always be my plight.
The compulsion to create,
is my ultimate fate.

Lesser Stars

What a torment it is
to hold the sun
within your soul
and be outshined
by lesser stars.

Futility

What's the use
    if all I have
    to protect
    myself with

Is an armor
    of glass
    and a paper
    sword?

Why must I
    keep fighting
    for the things I love
    when heartbreak
    is my reward?

The Things We Carry

I carry wounds
around with me
where there should
be scars.

I carry shadows
within me
where there once
were stars.

A Cruel Lesson

She looks at him with hopeful eyes
and wonders if she'll ever learn,
that fairy tales are all but lies
and not everyone is loved in return.

Body Image

When will I
be comfortable
in my own skin,
I wonder,

I fear I might
end up hating
a body,
whose only desire
is to be loved.

Skin Deep

She starves herself to look her best,
for all the boys she must impress.

He does not look at his reflection,
for fear of seeing his complexion.

To the pretty, young things walking tall,
what's it like to have it all?

A Necessary Evil

It would be easier and less painful for me
to not desire and pine for you this way.

So I taught myself to fall out of love
by finding reasons to hate you
every single f--king day.

Sweet Vengeance

You left me promises long ago,
dangled neatly in a row,

Above my head beyond all reach,
regardless of how I did beseech,

For you to give me but a sip,
your words remained beyond my grip.

And then you went and snipped it free,
said it wasn't meant to be,

I've stayed alive out of spite
to watch you eat your heart outright.

Your tears in mouthfuls I will drink-
Oh, vengeance will be sweet, I think.

Coping Mechanism

You're lucky the only thing I did to quiet
the demons in my head is write poetry,
that it was the only way I knew how to heal.

If words weren't my drug,
I'd find other deadlier ways to feel.

A Way Out

It's better to feel nothing,
        than to be miserable forever.

So I realized the only way
        to stop feeling bad,
        was to stop feeling altogether.

City Lights

Happy pills
    and vodka shots
    to drown away
    the lonely thoughts.

Cigarette smoke
    and city lights,
    a remedy
    for lonely nights.

Checklist

Angel dust and devil juice,
to numb the brain.
A happy face,
to hide the pain,

Rose-colored glasses,
over your eyes
to paint a world
of pretty lies.

A false promise or two
for a good night's sleep,
some dirty little secrets-
yours to keep.

Recover

You stole my heart
against my will,
then left me once
you've had your fill.

Now I am full
of dark distrust,
my flaming hope
as gray as dust.

Though time will tell
if I ever recover,
my heart will learn
to love another.

Worse for Wear

My feet have kissed valleys of thorn and walked on oceans of fire, taken me through gardens of bone and fields of glass,

But it is my heart that is the fragile one, you see. So be careful when you say those three words to me, 'cause I don't know how much longer it can last.

In the Meantime

I wonder if I'll ever find a soul strong enough to calm the chaos of my thoughts and draw the poison from my heart.

Until then I will have to be my own anchor, and poetry will be my cure. It's the only way to soothe the pain. It's the only way I can endure.

Practice Makes Perfect

Breathe in breathe out
then count to ten,
take two steps forward
and two again.
stand. sit. walk. smile.
I know that this may take awhile,
but take a breath and count to nine
and if they ask, just say you're fine.
Breathe in, breathe out
count one to four
take two steps back,
repeat once more.

Priority

Right now
    more than ever,
    I need to gather
    all the love
    I can find
    and pour it back
    into myself,

Because I will not
    waste it on the people
    who will give me
    nothing in return.

Warrior Spirit

A sword for a tongue,
fire in your belly,
stardust in your bones.

Eyes with the power
to melt hearts of stone.

Why do you believe them
when they say
that you're too weak
to fight your demons alone?

Saving Grace

Poetry has taught me
that broken people
are still capable
of creating beautiful things
even from the ugliest parts
of themselves.

Second Skin

I refuse to let love
turn me bitter.

But even if it has,
I will wear sweetness
like a second skin,

So that the ones who taste me
will know only
the nectar of my ways
and nothing else.

New Wounds

Your memories
    that come and go,
    that cut me deeper
    than a blade,

The shards of you
    that pierce me through,
    the secret wounds
    that they have made,

To take you out
    and stop the blood,
    the price that must
    be paid,

Now all I do
    is rise anew,
    and wait for every
    trace to fade.

Old Scars

The mark you left
        upon my soul
        I never will
        forget,

I know because
        your kiss will last
        like every
        past regret,

The things you did
        will stay with me
        but if I'd
        care to bet,

My life with you
        will fade right through
        as if we'd
        never met.

- Chapter III -

Always and Forever

Infinity

To hold the sea
in cups of tea,
and endless nights
in sips of wine,

Each moment shared
beyond compare,
my hand in yours
our souls entwined,

The stars that shine
inside your eyes,
as all the hours
fall behind,

Infinity with you
my dear,
the briefest
in my mind.

Till Death

Your heart may soon
    no longer remember,
    but my blood will sing
    your name forever

Your soul may find
    somebody new
    but my flame will always
    burn for you

Your love for me
    might fade with time,
    but I will love you
    till I die.

Against All Odds

No fearsome dragon
        or impenetrable tower
        or evil curse
        can break us,
        no stormy sea
        or siren song.

For we are one,
        like the moon and sun,
        and not even time
        can keep us apart
        for long.

Fleeting Moments

She was stardust
    in a sea of darkness,
    and I was a sunbeam
    in a stormy sky.

We were but
    fleeting moments
    in history,
    passing each other by.

Savory

Every time I get
a mouthful
of the sea,
I am reminded
of the taste
of your skin
and the savory nectar
of your love
on my tongue.

Sugar and Salt

Now that you
    have sipped
    the smile
    from my lips,
    and drunk the nectar
    of my kiss
    with your wine,

You must partake
    of these tears,
    my dear,
    and taste the sorrow
    in my brine.

Walking Contradiction

Boys like him were born
of sorrow and desire
in sunshine
and rain.

With a heart of ice
and a soul on fire,
and eyes alight
with hope and pain.

You wonder why it hurts
to love him
when you can't
even tell,

That he's
part angel,
part hell.

Paradox

She had a head
full of hurricanes,
and a heart
made of gold.

She held the darkness
in her veins,
but there's starlight
in her soul.

Inside Out

I am not what you think I am.
  I have wildfire for a soul
  and a kaleidoscope heart,
  there is ink in my veins
  where blood once flows
  and a universe in my head
  that no one knows.

Now cover me in human skin,
  can you tell what lies within?

Petals and Thorns

You only see
    the parts of me
    that blossom in the light.

When you don't know
    what I don't show
    the parts I've hidden out of sight.

You only feel as much
    as where I let you touch,
    unless your hands wander where they might.

Should you be too enchanted by my smell
    to notice where my monsters dwell,
    they might just leave a nasty bite.

Wild Things

Let's shed this meatsuit, my love;
peel off civilization from our skin
and become otherworldly beings,
if that's alright.

Let's make love beneath the sky
and howl at the stars,
even if it's just for tonight.

Wet Dreams

These painful thoughts
of pure delight,
that blur my sense
of wrong and right,

Are for all the things
that I have pined,
conjured from
my wicked mind,

Figments of desire
that come and go,
for all the ones
who do not know,

A good night's sleep
brings no respite,
from all the embers
they ignite,

But just this once,
to slake my thirst
I'll clear my pipes
before they burst.

Slow Burn

Teach me things I can't unlearn
        touch me, tease me, make me moan,

But don't deny me when I yearn
        to feel your lips against my own,

If you would let me take my turn
        I'll leave a kiss that melts through bone.

Goosebumps

The way he kisses me on the neck sends tingles down my spine, and makes the fine hairs on my skin stand on end, the sensation rippling through my body like a current; my bones melting at his very touch.

"Don't stop," I beg.

"I won't," he says.

Last Temptation

You gave me first
a glass of wine,
I told you then
that I was fine,

Then you made
for me a dish,
but I told you that
was not my wish,

But then you offered
me your lips
and I dared to take
the smallest sips.

When I said to you
I wanted more
you had me begging
on all fours.

One taste of you
and I was yours.

I Don't Love You

I don't love you, my dear, I never have. What I loved was how you carried moonlight in your teeth and constellations in your eyes.

How I can hear the ocean when I put my ear above your heart to listen to the waves crashing against your ribcage.

How your scent reminds me of lavender fields, as if God had planted a garden beneath your skin.

I don't love you, my dear, and that's a lie. It's the only truth I dare deny.

Eclipse

Maybe you're the sun, and maybe I'm the moon,
and maybe we were never meant to be,
but I swear one day we will collide,
and the stars will sigh with jealousy.

Ephemeral

Temporary people
    in temporary places,
    strangers' lips,
    on empty faces.

Fleeting moments
    and falling stars,
    bleeding wounds
    and fading scars.

But the memories
    of you and I,
    will stay with me
    until I die.

You and Me

I would be your butter,
        if you would be my bread.

I would be your pillow,
        if you would be my bed.

But I'd rather be your poetry,
        if only you would let me-

Get inside that pretty head.

Heart's Desire

If I could have one wish, my love,
do you know what I would ask?
It's not to own the stars above,
but have each moment last.

I'd make you mine for all my days
if it were ever in my power,
I'll love you right in every way
for every second of every hour.

If I could have one thing my dear,
do you know what it would be?
To have you here,
right next to me.

Yellow Brick Road

Lift me off
    take me far
    to other worlds
    where they are
    through munchkin towns
    past witches' den
    over rainbows
    then back again
    in ruby slippers
    with magic powers
    through poppy fields
    and emerald towers
    with flying monkeys
    and scarecrows too
    where wizards make
    your dreams come true,
    take me there
    where skies are blue.

Even if
    the only thing
    that's real
    is you.

Simple Pleasures

Smelling roses,
eating pie,
building castles
in the sky.

Writing poems
drinking tea,
having picnics
by the sea.

Watching dust motes
as they dance,
catching rainbows
in my hands.

True Colors

Love her darkness and her light
love her on her saddest day,
love her colors black and white
and all her shades of gray.

Love her when she's red with rage
and when she's feeling blue,
love her when she's all aglow
with all her brightest hue.

Love her yellow, green and orange
her pink and purple too,
for she trusts no other soul
to love her colors more than you.

Shades of You

There is an infinite
number of colors,

The pink of lips after kissing
the indigo of sleepless eyes,
the golden smile of daybreak,
the crimson blush of a soul.

Brushstrokes against
a sky of blue.

All of them, my favorite.
All of them,
you.

A Gentleman

His eyes, his smile,
    his suit and tie,
    the scent of him
    that makes you sigh.

A high class,
    high-end
    kinda guy.

Amazing in bed.
    Not a hair
    out of place
    on his head.

The Magician

What is this strange and wicked
magic that you weave,
from which I can find
neither freedom nor reprieve?

Your love is like a puzzle box;
a riddle with no clues.
It has me dancing on the rainbows
with sunshine in my shoes.

Tell me your secrets, my darling-
what makes you tick the way you do?
What is this power that you have,
that has me falling so in love with you?

Natural Phenomenon

You are not just a lightning bolt
that I can ground,
or another storm
that I can weather.

I'll always feel you
in my blood,
and that is where
you'll stay forever.

Earthly Dreams

Take me past the city lights,
        past the stars,
        and pale moonbeams.

Take me far away from here,
        my dear,
        beyond these earthly dreams.

Creatures of Habit

Morning cuddles,
breakfast in bed
coffee cups
and buttered bread,
making love,
with you instead.
Nine to five
and dinner at eight,
drinking wine,
washing plates.
Naughty games
at half past ten
making love
with you again.

Pillow Talk

You asked me what made my soul burn and my heart fly. I blushed and said,

"You,"

And smiled as you kissed me on the forehead.

Then I asked you the same thing. You pulled me closer into your arms and whispered,

"This."

Prized Possession

I gave to you what's left of me-
remnants of what others took.

The parts of me you'll never see-
the missing pages of my book.

I've never given my heart out before,
but with you, I'll take the chance.

Be careful where you keep it, dear,
for my heart is now within your hands.

Moonstruck

I adore everything about you darling; your sun-kissed hair, your star-filled eyes, your kisses on my neck, and your fingers on my skin. From your bourbon breath to your cigarette smoke.

Down to your wine-drenched lips and moonlit words and all the feelings they invoke.

Always and Forever

I will love you my dear
through rain and shine,
through sleet and snow,
through space and time,
past stormy sea
and stormy sky,
to worlds beyond
the naked eye,
with shooting stars
and shining moon,
to hell and back
just me and you.

Forever and always
here and now,
my lips on yours,
a solemn vow,
to walk with you
through frost and flame,
if you would vow
to do the same.

All for You

The secrets and the scars
        that I've been concealing,

The breaking and the mending,
        the hurting and the healing,

The things that I could never say,
        on this page, for you to find one day.

All these words
        the old and the new,

All my words.
        All for you.

Déjà vu

Little Flowers

Every petal that I've shed
is a sliver of hope, or a morsel of love,
as rain and wind ruffle me
relentlessly.

I brave through every storm
and weather through the hail,

In the end,
though I knew not then,
that cosmic forces would prevail,
my structure proved too frail.

What chance had I,
to contest, contradict or vie
against the otherworldly powers
reigning from their celestial towers
who care not for helpless little flowers?

Our Kind of Love

Your kisses burn through bone,
my skin scorched red and pink,
I feel your flesh against my own,
your fingers trace a hieroglyph
in an intricate design,
circles, diamonds, squares and lines,
that only you can decipher.
We coil like vipers,
serpentine.
I count your heartbeat,
seven... eight... nine.
I drink your breath like turpentine.
Burn me brighter with your power,
I feel our fire down my spine.

Three Words

Blood of red, veins of blue,
my head is filled with thoughts of you.
I gave my heart, it broke in two,
roses and violets and getting screwed.
The hurt I felt, the days I rued,
this oddly feels like déjà vu.

Doppelganger

More often now than then
although I don't remember when
I'd feel a whisper near my ear
words and sights that seemed too queer,
and other times, I can't recall
the thoughts that came before the rest,
for they won't come at my behest.
'Twas as if my mind's a wall
or miles and miles of empty halls,
where voices echo, in tongues and riddles
and phantoms play with drums and fiddles.
While imps and sprites cavort in the air,
and I'm imprisoned in this lair
that I have forged unknowingly,
from the cleavage in my mind.
My alter ego's world in me
within its cages, I'm confined.

Fragile

I came to you like moths to firelight,
like iron dust to magnetite.
But every soul that fluttered by,
who mistook the venom on your fingers for nectar
has now become a broken specter,
And here I am subjugated within your palm,
my wounds immune to any balm,
except the poultice that you brew
from devil's-vine and scorpion wine
that sealed my cuts like magic glue.
But from that day on I knew,
that though you'll mend me if I break,
my shards were yours to give or take.

Mirror Image

Not many things in nature
can change the old for new,
and of all the creatures that are able,
as gods and spirits of ancient fable,
we are not among these few.

Oh, how I wish to peel the external,
and by some power,
either divine or infernal,
replace
my dismal face
for a fairer complexion.
That I may cease to hate
my own reflection.

Dysphoria

Crimson imps scream with glee,
demons come in pairs of three.
My mind's become a maze of thorn,
home to beasts of fang and horn.
I run in circles, batting sprites
chasing tails and fairy lights.
Trapped in bars of flame and frost
and gates of death that can't be crossed.
Seconds echo, hours chime,
I lose all track of space and time.
The Sandman comes to end the wait,
sleep arrives, a minute late.

Fine Print

She knew not of the fairy's trick,
and her troubles were gone
with a swish and a flick.
The wand was waved,
and a spell was cast.
But as soon as she thought
that her fortunes would last,
she fell in love and married her beau.

But little did, poor Cinderella know,
of the consequences of her deed,
the likes of which her godmother
had decreed,
but had failed to mention-
as was her cruel deception;

What she had to sacrifice.
Her dresses turned to rags,
her steed became mice.
And the eternal summer
that followed her head,
till the day she was wed,
turned into a curse of snow and ice.

Mixed Signals

Feathers of frost, they tickle my nose
and turn my moist cheeks
a deeper shade of pink.

The truth is, this timid act
is just for show,
and I'm much more mischievous
than you think.

I hurled a ball of ice at your face
before you could even blink.
I watched you smile your wicked smile,
and wink.

And the next thing I knew,
a war had ensued,
when all I had wanted,
was for you to ask me out for a drink.

Plot Twist

The damsel watched as princes burned
because they did not know or had not learned
as droves of knights were scorched and charred
by the flame of her fearsome guard
that he was just protecting her you see
and she's not waiting for true love's kiss
for he was her beloved and she was his.

Prescription

I take you every morning with my vitamins,
with a glass of wine and toast.
What we had was tragic, and magic,
even when I overdosed
on sorrow, lust, and caffeine,
as was my routine.

I could not help but reflect
on the cause and effect
of what you were doing
to my cerebral chemistry.
Your spells and songs and poetry.
Your witchcraft, your deviltry.

When I could not fathom the mystery,
what I pondered on instead,
were the trying days that lay ahead.

I realized the moment I abstained
and took their poison for my pain,
that this emptiness cannot be fed.

Unwritten

You were the book I never wrote;
 an unheard quote,
 a secret note,
 a song, unsung,
 the rhymes on my tongue,
 the sentences lingering,
 at the back of my throat

You were my myth, my story,
 my shame, my glory,
 my antidote, my affliction,
 my words, my diction,
 my fact,
 my fiction.

EPILOGUE

Poetry is too ingrained
in my brain,
so I will not abstain.

I will write
till my hair turns white,
I'll take this pleasure with the pain.

Incantations

Truth Spell

"SECRETS UNRAVEL,
WORDS UNBIND
SAY WHAT'S TRULY
ON YOUR MIND,

JOY AND SADNESS
HOPE AND FEAR
SPEAK THE TRUTH
FOR ALL TO HEAR."

Beauty Spell

"LET SAND BE PEARL,
LET CLAY BE GOLD,
LET NEW LIFE AWAKEN
FROM THE ASHES OF THE OLD.
APHRODITE, I CALL ON YOUR POWER
HEAR MY COMMAND
LET ME BLOSSOM LIKE A FLOWER,
AND BE FAIREST IN THE LAND."

Lucky Charm Spell

"SILVER PENNY
IN MY HAND,
BRING ME BLESSINGS
WHERE I STAND.
DISPEL MY TROUBLES
QUICK AND FAST,
BEFORE THEY EVEN
COME TO PASS.
A STROKE OF LUCK
TO SEE ME THROUGH,
GOOD FORTUNE FLOWS
THROUGH ALL I DO."

Memory Spell

"MEMORIES PAST, I NOW ERASE
OF WHAT I NOW MENTION
LEAVE NO TRACE.
BUT TO KEEP THESE EVENTS
AS AUTHENTIC AS REQUIRED
FILL IN THE BLANKS
AS THEY WOULD HAVE TRANSPIRED."

Knowledge Spell

"FLAME OF WISDOM
INTO MY THOUGHTS IGNITE,
BRAND INTO MY MEMORY
THE WORDS I READ THIS NIGHT.

HERB OF REMEMBRANCE
WARMED BY FIRE
INFUSE INTO MY MIND
THE KNOWLEDGE I DESIRE."

Obedience Spell

"LIKE PUPPETS ON A STRING,
LIKE PUTTY IN MY HANDS,
LET THOSE WHO HEAR MY VOICE
BEND TO MY COMMANDS.
WITH EVERY WORD
THAT LEAVES MY LIPS,
I'LL HAVE YOU AT
MY BECK AND CALL,
TO SERVE MY NEEDS
BOTH GREAT AND SMALL.
FROM THIS DAY FORTH
YOU'LL FALL IN LINE,
TO EVERY TWISTED
WHIM OF MINE."

Youth Spell

"THE PASSING YEARS
HAVE NOT BEEN KIND,
SO LET THE HANDS
OF TIME REWIND,

OLD AGE BEARS
A HEAVY COST,
RESTORE THE YOUTH
THAT I HAVE LOST."

Clean Slate Spell

"TRAGIC CHAPTERS
TORN AND BURNED
LET A BRAND NEW PAGE
BE TURNED
WITH FRESH STARTS
AND OPEN HEARTS.

SINS FORGOTTEN,
FAULTS FORGIVEN
LET THESE MEMORIES
BE REWRITTEN.
DARK GRUDGES
THAT WON'T RESET-
NOW FORGIVE AND
FORGET."

Love Spell

"LOVE IS FICKLE
LOVE IS BLIND,
SO TAKE HIS HEART
AND MAKE IT MINE."

TO REVERSE:

"LOVE IS CRUEL
LOVE IS KIND,
RETURN HIS LOVE
MY SPELL, UNBIND."

Quick Spell

"WHEN TIME IS MOVING
FAR TOO FAST,
AND YOU DON'T WANT
TO FINISH LAST,
COMMAND THE CLOCK
TO FREEZE IN PLACE,
SO YOU CAN STAND
TO WIN THE RACE.
FLEET OF FOOT
TO WORK YOUR DEED
HALF THE TIME
AT TWICE THE SPEED."

Twisted Tales

THE CRUEL, CRUEL SEA

Once upon a time, in the deepest, darkest depths of the ocean, lived a little mermaid, who was also, quite unfortunately, a little different from the rest of her kind.

Where her sisters had glorious emerald and ruby scales, and locks the color of coral and gold, Serena had a tail that was as black as night, and hair as white as snow. She had crawled out of her egg, a terrifying looking creature.

But it wasn't what she looked like on the outside that was the only thing other merfolk feared about her, for Serena also possessed a gift that very few mermaids had, a dangerous and powerful ability that flowed invisibly within her cold, dark blood.

Magic.

Even as a hatchling, Serena would unintentionally stir storms with her weeping, sending mortals' ships to their watery doom and flooding nearby human villages. But when her heart was all aglow with bliss, undersea flowers would bloom wherever she swam, leaving a garden of colors in her wake.

Her parents had forbidden her to use her gifts, calling them unholy. But Serena had silently honed them in secret, to the point where she could spin whirlpools in the water with a flick of her wrist, and transform fish into seaweed with a snap of her fingers.

But as the centuries went by without the love and acceptance of her own family, Serena finally fled from her home in the city of pearls where she was born, to the loneliest part of the sea, close to the shore where no mermaid has ever ventured.

Serena had found an old abandoned cave, which she made her new home. And for years that was where she lived, with nothing but the silly crabs and the talkative seabirds as her loyal companions.

But that was all about to change.

One stormy day, as the temperamental sea chased all the sailors and fishers back to shore, Serena was distraught to find a stray boat taking shelter in her beloved cave.

She had spent the day collecting treasures with which to decorate her abode and returned only to find one of the land-walkers resting on her favorite stone perch. Serena was about to send a bolt of magic at him before he turned around.

They both stared at each other in mutual bewilderment, both rendered speechless at the sight of the other. Serena's anger melted as she met his gaze.

He was the most beautiful human she had ever seen.

This mortal man may be nothing more than a fisher, judging by his old boat and the net that rested within it, but her mermaid eyes saw nothing but divine perfection.

He did not recoil with horror at her presence, which many mortals were known to do when they happen to catch a glimpse of a real mermaid on the surface, rare an occurrence though it may be.

Serena swam towards him, her white hair trailing behind her like the gossamer vestiges of a ghost. He approached her just as cautiously and knelt by the water to meet her.

"Hello," he said. Like all mermaids, Serena could understand all the languages of living things, even the barbarous tongue of men.

"Hello," she replied. "What are you called?" She asked. The mortal man placed his palm on his heart.

"I am Dimitri, and you? What is your name?" he asked, his eyes blazing with curiosity.

"I have many names, but you may call me Serena."

"Are you... a siren?" he asked. In the language of the land-walkers, sirens were what they called her kind, but it was not the most accurate word to describe what she was. Too kind to argue, Serena simply nodded.

"I have never seen a siren before, but many do not even believe you exist," he said. "Are there more of you?" Again, Serena nodded, too mesmerized by his beautiful golden eyes to offer a better answer. His gaze turned to the sky outside and then back to her.

"I must go," he said reluctantly. "If I do not bring more fish, my family will starve," he said.

Not wanting the human to leave, Serena abruptly said:

"I can help you with the fish,"

"How?" Dimitri asked, puzzled.

"Just watch," she said. Serena swam back a little deeper into the water and closed her eyes. Beneath the surface, her fingers crackled with magic. Within a few seconds, hundreds of fish flooded the cave, their tails thrashing against one another, disoriented by the strange power that called them there.

"This is my gift to you mortal, a token of my friendship," she said, her heart fluttering with warm happiness at the sight of his delighted expression.

"All this for me? What do you ask in return?" Dimitri asked.

"Come and see me every day, and tell me of your adventures on land, and I will give you more fish than you could ever dream," Serena promised.

"You do not need to give me fish, but may I come see you anyway?" Dimitri asked, wading into the water after her as the fish splashed around them. She didn't swim away when he took her hand in his.

"You may do as you please," she said, looking away, pretending not to be overjoyed at his proposition. From that day on, they became friends, a mortal man from the human world, and a mermaid girl from the cold, watery land beneath the waves.

***

Dimitri would visit her every day after that, and Serena would patiently await his arrival at sundown. It became the one thing she would look forward to each morning as she woke.

During the day, Serena would often secretly find his boat among a dozen others out in the sea, only to send schools of fish his way, to hasten his return to her side. Dimitri became the only creature who could comfort her silent sorrow.

He would always come bearing gifts from the mortal world, anything he could spare with what little fortune he made: some delicious human food, wooden toys, books, clothes, and jewelry. But what Serena enjoyed most of all were the candles and lamps, for she had never seen fire before.

One day, he brought her something truly enchanting.

"I brought you a gift," he said, and unearthed a large, magnificent lily that he had hidden in a box.

He tucked the flower behind Serena's ear, and it cast its wonderful fragrance all over her. It was not at all like the undersea flowers she was used to. It was delicate and would not at all survive the crushing weight of the sea.

But that was what made it more precious. The flower was ephemeral, just like everything else in the human world. Mortal lives were so fragile and brief, whereas mermaids could live for thousands of years and still be in the prime of their youth.

She thanked him for his gift, and he kissed the back of her hand; his warm human lips, a friendly flame against her cold, wet flesh.

Serena wondered what cruel punishment awaited her back in the city of pearls if her family knew that she had been consorting with a land-walker.

In all her centuries of life, Serena had never met face to face with a mortal, let alone conversed with one. But she had felt more loved and at home with Dimitri than she ever did amongst her own kind.

Dimitri told her all about himself, his past, and his dreams. His hopes and fears. The secrets of his strange mortal life. And Serena did the same. They were both fascinated by each other's stories, and soon their friendship blossomed into something more.

They confessed their feelings one fateful evening as Serena laid in his arms.

"Serena, I have lived by the sea my entire life, but it seems lately, I find that it is more enchanting than ever before. I dream of the waves every night when I sleep, and hear the ocean when I am awake."

"I, too, dream of the land, the feel of the sand between my fingers, the touch of the hot air on my skin, the blazing golden sun above my head. I dream of light in the darkness of my sleep," Serena said.

"I believe the sea has stolen my heart," Dimitri said. Serena turned around to face the mortal man with whom she was desperately smitten and said. "I believe you have stolen the heart of the sea as well," she said.

They shared their first kiss on that night, a gift they would both remember until their dying day.

***

But Fate was a cruel mistress, and she cast her envious eye upon the star-crossed lovers.

Dimitri had stopped coming to the cave one day, to Serena's dismay.

But Serena dismissed his absence as an unavoidable consequence of being a dutiful son. Parents oftentimes demanded quite unreasonable errands of their offspring.

But weeks sped by and her heart grew cold without the warmth of Dimitri's company. It was on the thirteenth day that she decided to tap into the darkest parts of her magic, to bring about a powerful enchantment that would allow her to walk on the earth.

As a mortal.

Serena scoured the ocean floor for the ingredients she would need for her dark spell, and at sundown, far beneath the waters before a great stone cauldron, she set her plan in motion.

"Heart of a nixie, wings of a sprite, blood of kelpie, black as night," the mermaid recited as she tossed each ingredient into the depths of the stone pot. The potion glowed with a sinister purple light.

Serena raised her hands above her head and unleashed her forbidden powers, singing an incantation that would fulfil her deepest, darkest desire.

"Ancient ones of the cruel sea,
By these offerings, hear my command.
Let me walk where mortals be,
Where the ocean leaves the sand.
I give my soul, o Dark Gods, to thee,
And my wretched heart to this man.
That I may be with he,
Who lives and breathes upon the land."

Her voice thundered throughout the cave, sending ripples across the water and awakening the ancient, slumbering forces of the sea. Serena's hands crackled with magic lightning.

An evil green whirlwind burst forth from her stone cauldron and engulfed Serena within its tempestuous embrace. She disappeared into the depths of the wild and powerful magic, and surrendered herself to the throes of an unnatural metamorphosis.

The spell carried the mermaid out of her cave, upwards through the water, and relinquished her to the surface. Serena was hurled from the sea onto the beach, her tail missing, and in its place, a pair of human legs.

Serena marveled at her new appendages. They were not at all graceful or fast, but felt clumsy and cumbersome under her weight. Moving through the harsh, dry world of the humans was confusing, when she had gotten so used to the smooth, liquid atmosphere of the sea.

Using her magic once more, she transformed a pile of seaweed nearby into a set of human clothes and dressed herself in them, before leaving the cave and trying desperately to navigate the ground with her new human feet.

The skin of her soles burned where they touched the earth, an unforeseen consequence of her spell, payment for her passage into a world in which she did not belong. Every step she took felt like she was walking on coals.

But Serena was determined to find her beloved, and did so by using a magical conch she had enchanted with her own blood.

"Show me where my heart resides," she whispered to it, and it whispered back, telling her where she will find what she most desired.

It would have taken her a mere moment to find her quarry if she were not so enchanted by the little mortal village in which she had found herself. The land-walkers were a busy folk, and there was not a single one who was not either walking, running, dancing or otherwise absorbed in some kind of activity.

Curious sights and smells tickled her senses, and for a moment she wondered what life would be like as a human. It was no doubt a painful and brief existence filled with sorrow and suffering, but between those dark times flickered the fleeting moments of joy and happiness that somehow made everything worthwhile.

The conch glowed faintly in Serena's hand and there, near a fountain, was Dimitri, his hand interlocked with those of a girl. They appeared to be occupied in deep conversation.

A surge of anger erupted from Serena, and her magic burst forth, swirling invisibly through the oblivious crowd. The spell sent a curl of water from the fountain towards the girl, drenching her from head to toe.

Soaked and ashamed, the girl fled, leaving Dimitri all alone. Serena marched towards him, but the sight of his handsome face quelled her rage. His eyes widened in surprise and joy, not with guilt.

"Serena?" he asked, looking at her feet in astonishment. "You have legs? How?" He approached her, but she held up her hand.

"It does not matter, but you must explain yourself," she asked. "Who was that girl and why have you not come to see me in weeks?"

The light on Dimitri's face faded into a gloomy shadow, and he gently took both her hands in his.

"Forgive me, Serena, I was going to come and find you, to explain, but with the wedding preparations..."

"Wedding?" Serena asked in disbelief.

"My parents," Dimitri began. "They have arranged for my marriage with a nobleman's daughter."

Serena's blood turned to ice at these words.

"She comes from a good family, a wealthy family, and it would be a mark of dishonor to refuse the proposal."

"So that girl is your bride-to-be, then?" Serena asked, untangling her fingers from Dimitri's grasp.

"Do you love her?"

"No," Dimitri said, looking away. "She is quite smitten with me, you see, but I am not in love with her. But her parents have offered to give mine a comfortable life, a life full of gold coins."

"And that is what your heart desires? To shower your burdensome family with riches?" Serena asked. "I can bring you all the gold you need, my poor sweet human, you need only ask." she said viciously.

"Gold to merfolk is like sand to mortals." She explained. "They fall down on our cities beneath the water from sunken ships like rain. You do not need to imprison yourself in this loveless union out of duty."

"I cannot ask you to do that, I have made a promise long ago and promises cannot be forsaken," Dimitri said, with pain and regret in his voice.

"What about your promises to me?" Serena asked, her eyes filling with salty tears, a bitter reminder of the home she had sacrificed in the name of love.

"I cannot give you the life you want. I wish I could join you in your world, but who will take care of my family? And I will not ask you to join me in mine, for it is a cruel and harsh world that grinds a man to dust before he is even old enough to marry."

"You pluck reasons out of the air, like flowers from a garden," she accused. "I wish you a happy life, Dimitri," and with that she fled from his presence, away from the bright and noisy human town, leaving a trail of tears behind her.

That night, in the depths of her cave, she cast another spell, one that would allow her to return to the cold, merciless ocean.

"Oceanus, Poseidon, Proteus. Gods of the sea, hear my plea, my true form I now reclaim, send me back from whence I came," she chanted. But from the depths of the water arose, not her salvation, but a grotesque creature that seemed to change forms ever so often, as if it had trouble deciding what shape to take.

"I am a messenger of the sea gods," the creature said.

"I wish to return to the sea, return my mermaid form," Serena said to the ancient, nightmarish entity before her, a writhing, shifting mass of limbs, eyes, and creature parts that seemed to pulse with sinister power.

"You have sacrificed a precious birthright to be in this wretched world; the price for your return will not be so easily paid."

"What must I do?" she asked.

The creature held out one of its many arms, and an old, rusty blade appeared from beneath its skin. It carved itself out of the creature's flesh, leaving a gruesome wound that closed instantly.

"Take this knife," the creature instructed. Serena obeyed, fearful of the toll that she must pay for her safe passage back to her birthworld.

"In order to return to the ocean, you must take the life of that which you love most in this world, and cast its heart into the sea," the creature said. "That is your payment, child." It uttered one last time before slowly descending back into the water.

Confounded by such a heartless, bloodthirsty request, Serena missed her chance to ask for a different sacrifice. Anything but the one that she was asked to make.

But she had no other choice. Live out the rest of her brief, human life without Dimitri by her side, or return to the ocean where she belonged.

That night, as Dimitri lay sleeping, Serena crept into his room, knife in hand. She stood beside him at the edge of his bed, her heart twisting in anguish. With trembling hands and tears in her eyes, Serena drew the dagger above her head and brought the blade swiftly down upon Dimitri's heart.

***

The next morning, Serena found herself on the edge of the beach, watching the sun rise. She would return to the sea today, one way or the other. Nearby in the water, floating innocently, was the knife that was given to her the night before.

Out in the distance, Serena could hear faint footsteps

approaching. Her head turned towards the sound.

It was Dimitri, running in her direction as if his life depended on it.

"Serena! I thought I'd never see you again," he said, stopping next to her to catch his breath.

"I looked for you last night, in the cave, but you weren't there."

Serena felt a small, sharp twinge deep within her as she rose to meet him, but replied nonetheless with a bright smile. She would not let him see her tears.

"I took a walk down the beach, to be alone with my thoughts," she said. They stood facing each other on the beach. Not a single soul in sight.

She had brought the blade so close to his beating heart the night before, but stopped herself before she could harm him. Serena could not bring herself to do it. After all, how could she destroy the one thing she truly loved in this world?

"I was going to come find you," she began. "To say goodbye." The joy bled from Dimitri's face.

"Goodbye?" he asked.

"Yes, it is time I returned home," Serena said, with a sad, wistful smile.

"Back home?" he asked in confusion. "To the city of pearls?"
Serena swallowed back her sorrow and nodded. "Yes, the city."

"Thank you for all that you've done for me, for showing me what love feels like," she said and gently touched his cheek.

"I wish I can pay your kindness with coins, but all I have is my gratitude."

"It was an honor to know you Serena, my goddess from the sea," Dimitri said, as he put his palm above her hand. His eyes welled with tears.

"I wish things could be different, that we could be together," he said.

"Forgive me for causing you so much pain."
"Of course I forgive you, I love you," she said.

Serena took Dimitri in her arms one last time and cherished every second, wanting nothing more than to remain frozen forever in the warmth and comfort of his embrace. They shared one final kiss, and she opened her shattered, mangled heart to the sweet and exquisite pain of loving him, knowing that he could never be hers.

"You will visit me in the future, yes?" Dimitri asked.
"Of course," she lied, knowing that this was the last time they would ever see each other again.

As they disentwined, Serena walked away, looking back one last time at the man she loved and raised her hand in a gesture of farewell, which he reciprocated. She burned the image of his smile into her memory, an immortal token of her joy, that she will carry with her till the day she died.

That evening, from the edge of a tall cliff, Serena cast herself into the roiling sea and surrendered her body and soul to the cruel depths from whence she came, and embraced the promise of the sweet release that was about to come. As she crashed into the water, the waves claimed her, sending her corpse to its watery grave.

***

Alas, the death she wished for did not come, for the sea gods who had granted her a human form were not pleased with her treachery. They revived her, brought life back into her bones, and transformed her into a creature that was once thought to live only within the fevered nightmares of merfolk.

In the place of a mermaid's tail, they transformed her human legs into tentacles, eight black limbs that looked as if she was attached to a writhing mass of sea serpents, as punishment for her trespasses.

As soon as she awakened and witnessed her new form for the first time, the monstrosity that she had become, she summoned the sea gods out of rage. In their place came the messenger; the nameless, shape-shifting sea creature with a hundred faces and a hundred arms.

"Why?!" Serena asked. "Why have they spared me? Given me this form?"

"You have not paid your debt, child. The price for your return was the heart of the thing you loved most in this world."

"But this is not what I wanted! I never wanted to return to the sea, not if it meant killing an innocent mortal man."

"But you did want this. Why else would you let the ocean take your miserable, worthless life?" said the sea spirit. Serena had no answer for it, but all that was unspoken was already said.

"As punishment for failing to live up to your end of the bargain, you will be sentenced to live out five thousand years in this monstrous form,"

"Do with your time as you please, but know this, you will never see the surface, or feel the sun on your skin until the day you perish."

Serena felt the last vestiges of warmth and longing bleed out of her body, leaving behind nothing but a cold, dead heart.

"If you think you can use your magic to return what you have lost, think again," the creature said. "Your powers can only be used in the service of others and never for yourself. You may try, but it will be for naught. You will never again feel what it is like to be human, or walk amongst mortals." And with that, the messenger vanished in a dark, evil cloud, never to return.

Devastated at the injustice of her fate, Serena vowed to bring despair to any merfolk who dared to dream of the mortal world or desire to be a part of it. She would show them the error of their ways, even if it meant their demise.

If she had to suffer for five thousand years, so must the world, and she would start her campaign of cruelty here, in her dark little corner of the sea.

From that day on, she fashioned herself a new name, a name she knew would strike fear in the hearts of merfolk for generations to come.

Ursula.

***

Ariel had never been to this part of the sea before, but the eels who found her weeping near the ruins of her secret chamber had instructed her to go to the forbidden cave at the darkest depths of Dead Man's Trench.

She had heard stories about this place, but had never dared to venture any further than the boundaries of the kingdom in which she resided. Her father, the king, would be mad if he found out where she was going.

But it was his fault to begin with. He never should have unleashed his childish wrath upon her beloved treasure trove of objects from the mortal realm. Her secret museum of the world above was now but a memory.

As Ariel approached the entrance to the fabled cave where legend tells lived a sea witch who could grant you anything you desired, she was suddenly struck by a strange fear. Discouraged by second thoughts at the sight of the pitch-black abyss that lay ahead, the young mermaid was about to turn back when a voice stopped her.

"Leaving so soon, dear?"

It echoed across the water and chilled her to the bone. Ariel felt as if the darkness itself was speaking to her.

"Hello?"

A figure appeared out of the shadows, a beautiful woman with long silver hair, violet eyes, and eight black tentacles in the place of a mermaid's tail.

"Hello," Ariel began, her voice shaking with fear.

"I-I was...wondering if you could help me," Ariel asked, overwhelmed by the fearsome sight of the legendary sea witch before her.

"My dear, sweet child, that's what I do. That's what I live for," Ursula said and wrapped one arm across Ariel's shoulder.

The young mermaid followed the sea witch into the mouth of her cave, unaware of the horrible fate that would soon befall her and all those who sought the aid of the mad sorceress who lived in the deepest depths of the darkest sea.

Out in the distance, two eels cackled gleefully, happy to serve another poor, unfortunate soul to their cruel, vengeful master.

The Dragon's Secret

Centuries ago, in an age long forgotten by man, lived the legend of a prince, a princess, a prophecy, and a kingdom ravaged by a great beast from the sky.

"We must do something to end this terror," the king said after yet another one of the human settlements under his protection was destroyed by the fire of the fearsome monster, whose wings could cast a shadow over an entire village.

"We must slay the beast and put an end to its madness," said the prince, a rebellious, hot-blooded young man who was eager to prove his mettle and his might before the great council of knights and warriors.

"You are much too young to go charging after that monster, and to think, my only heir to the kingdom," said the king. "I will leave this mission to our loyal soldiers."

"But father..."

"Enough, Philip, you are to stay within the palace. I have tasked every guard to make sure you do not step foot outside these grounds," the king decreed.

"Yes, father," said the prince. But he had other ideas in mind.

Killing the beast would truly be a mark of honor, but there was simply more to it than that. According to the words of an ancient oracle, the dragon had once captured a beautiful princess and put her in an enchanted sleep.

Anyone who slayed the dragon and rescued the sleeping princess with true love's kiss will be blessed with good fortune and endless wealth.

And Prince Philip's crumbling kingdom was in desperate need of both, especially with enemies from the north stalking the borders of their land, ready to strike at any moment of weakness.

Philip believed in the prophecy with all his heart, and his father, who did not, thought him a fool for believing in superstitious bedtime stories told to little children by their mothers.

Even if there was no great boon or a princess waiting to be rescued, dragons were known to be quite fond of gold. And there was no telling how much treasure the great monster had amassed over the centuries.

Gold could easily turn the tides of the silent war that was slowly brewing between the two rival kingdoms.

So, the next morning as the first battalion departed to The Black Mountain, home of the Great Dragon, Philip climbed out his bedroom window in full armor, unbeknownst to the guards stationed outside his door.

The prince stole a horse from the stables and stealthily pursued the congregation of soldiers and knights, making sure to remain hidden until they arrived at their destination.

Philip watched from the shadow of the trees as the small army entered the ruins of the castle in which dwelled the fearsome dragon. It was not long before he heard the sounds of fighting.

Steel blades clanking uselessly against impenetrable skin, screams of death as fire met flesh. He could not bear to hear it any longer. Prince Philip drew his sword from its sheath and rushed headlong into the danger, knowing it would be his dying act. He would lay down his life to save his kingdom.

It was, after all, his duty.

But the prince was too late. Carnage and tragedy awaited the young prince as he entered the great hall of the castle. Severed limbs, charred corpses and broken weapons were scattered all around.

He did not hope to survive this. His father was right after all, he was much too young and inexperienced to be fighting a dragon, especially when a dozen other more skilled fighters had failed.

Philip caught a glimpse of a large barbed tail disappearing into the shadows. He at least had the element of surprise. The dragon must have thought that it had won.

The prince crept along the shadows, squinting in the darkness to see where the dragon went. Out in the distance, a voice echoed.

"Please, kind sir, please help me." Unable to believe his ears, the prince ran towards the fabled princess, and found her sitting on a throne in a grand room with a high ceiling that was illuminated with the light of a hundred torches that lined the stone walls.

All around him were scattered mountains of gold coins, jewels, chests full of diamonds and all manner of precious things that could make a pirate weep with joy.

From where he stood, he could see that the princess was shrouded, her face hidden behind a purple veil. There was a thicket of roses surrounding the princess, imprisoning her in an impenetrable wall of thorns.

Prince Philip approached the princess slowly, his eyes darting left and right for any sign of the monster which he had come to slay.

He then began slicing the branches with his sword, leaving petals, thorns and splinters of bark and wood in his wake. Once the path was cleared, he approached the throne.

"Princess, you must come with me, I will take you home," he whispered, extending a hand towards the princess. But she did not move.

"Hurry princess, we must leave, before the dragon returns," Prince Philip coaxed once more, placing his hand over the princess' own. He recoiled in horror as the silhouette of the shrouded princess collapsed into a pile of bones and dust. A clever decoy for a foolish prince.

A deep, dangerous laugh echoed throughout the treasure room.

Just as Philip turned to face his cunning adversary, the dragon's large head reared from the shadows, and a shower of green smoke escaped its mouth, enveloping the prince in a cloud of venom.

When it dissipated, he found that he could no longer move, his limbs frozen as if his bones had turned to lead. His sword slipped from his grasp and fell onto the stone floor with a resounding clang.

Prince Philip was paralyzed.

He awaited his demise, as the dragon emerged from its hiding place. The prince's eyes widened in astonishment as he saw the great creature slowly transform into a man. Talons turned into fingers, and scales turned into skin.

Clothes miraculously materialized over its changing shape.

In its human form, the dragon was handsome and young-looking. He had long black hair that slipped just past his shoulders and bright green eyes, the color of emeralds, with slits for pupils. His ears were slightly pointed. The dragon was clad in leather trousers and a blood-red tunic that was unbuttoned at the neck, revealing his smooth, muscular chest.

The dragon flashed the frozen prince a triumphant smile and sauntered towards him with his hands clasped behind his back. He circled his prisoner, as if admiring a work of art.

The dragon approached Philip from behind and placed both his hands over the prince's shoulders, and put his face close to the prince's ear.

"Hmmmm... royal blood," the dragon said as he sniffed the prince's hair.

"... and handsome too. I've never had a prince before," he said as he caressed the prince's neck seductively.

"I was wondering when you'd come, Prince Philip, I've been picking knights off my teeth for months," the dragon said. The prince was rendered silent from his fear and from the dragon's strange poison.

"You probably think breathing fire is the only thing I can do, tsk tsk," the dragon said, feigning disappointment. "A dragon has many powers, and petrifying his enemy with poisoned breath is one among many."

The dragon continued inspecting the prince, turning the prince around to face him. He lifted Philip's chin with his finger and gazed directly into the frightened prince's eyes.

"My venom is flowing through your blood as we speak, bending you to my will," the dragon explained. "You have no choice but to follow my orders, whether you want to or not."

The prince could only stare into the dragon's emerald eyes as he fought to break through whatever cursed enchantment that had ensnared him. But the dragon suddenly came to a realization, as if ashamed by an impure thought.

"Oh, how rude of me, I haven't even introduced myself," said the handsome and cruel dragon.

He took several steps back and dramatically presented a deep and flamboyant bow.

"Your Highness," the dragon drawled pretentiously.
"My name... is Maleficent,"

The prince swallowed his terror. The dragon, whose name was Maleficent, took him by the hand and led him towards the throne. With a single powerful breath, the dragon scattered the pile of bones that lay upon it.

"Do you like my little decoy?" Maleficent asked. "The princess has been dead for years, even before my time," he said, laughing.

"I still can't believe how many of you silly little humans believe in that fairy tale I've conjured," Maleficent said as he set himself down upon the throne and made Philip sit on his lap, like a marionette with all its strings cut.

"Behold, my dear prince." He said, gesturing to the sea of gold before them. "My kingdom of stolen treasures."

Maleficent looked at the prince.

"Are you entertained?" the dragon asked. He laughed at the prince's silence.

"Very well, let me tell you my story then," he declared finally. "It's not every day I get to meet a prince."

Prince Philip sat like a stone statue on the dragon's lap, unable to protest or escape.

"Well, you see we have much in common," he began. "I was just like you once, a prince, the heir to a great kingdom that was the envy of all other kingdoms in the continent. You may not have heard of me, it was such a long time ago and my throne has been taken by another king, a filthy usurper who had brought ruin and devastation to my home," he said.

"Do you want to know who that king is, my dear prince?" The prince could only look at his captor helplessly, the dragon's enchanted venom rendering him speechless.

"It's your father." The dragon revealed finally. Philip felt a curl of anger rise out of him. Lies. His father was a good man.

"Yes, the man who raised, fed and loved you, is the villain of my story," the dragon said. "Shall I start from the beginning?"

Maleficent did not wait to hear the prince's reply.

"It all began 50 years ago when I was still just a boy, old enough to not be a child, but still too young to be called a man.

"My father's kingdom was a prosperous nation, but he soon sought to form an alliance with the neighboring countries, to expand his influence and share his resources." The dragon's eyes glazed over, as if recalling a fond memory.

"Though I loved my father dearly, he was also a gullible man. He trusted too easily and believed in a magical world where there was no war, or famine or hardship where everyone would work towards the betterment of their fellow man," he continued.

"Alas, his dream was but a fool's wish, and he paid the price for his innocence dearly.

"I learned this much later in my life, from the mouth of a witch, that on the night of the peace treaty, a neighboring king had poisoned my father's chalice with a curse, a curse that was meant to start a war.

"You see, this king envied the prosperity of our country much more than all the other monarchs who attended the treaty. He wanted a reason to wage war with my father to steal his treasured gold mines and fertile crops for his own dying kingdom.

"But as luck would have it, my foolish young self, who had never had a sip of wine, craved for a taste. So I stole a mouthful from my father's chalice when he wasn't looking.

"It seemed as though your dear father did not know exactly what the curse would do because he, as many others, fled in horror as I transformed into a great beast right before their eyes.

"I was still a young man you see, and did not understand what was happening to me, or why the guards were suddenly swinging at me with their swords.

"Frightened, I fled from my home, crashing through the stone walls of the great hall as if they were made of cheap parchment. I found my wings and flew for the first time as a dragon.

"That was the last time I saw my father, or my kingdom, for I had found refuge in a large mountain. I had resolved to starve myself to death than hurt another living soul, but dragons are quite indestructible, you see. I spent decades sleeping my hunger away."

Prince Philip listened to the story against his will. He could only pray for someone to come and rescue him, but they would need a large army to subdue such a formidable foe. But he had little hope that anyone would come.

Maleficent continued, oblivious to the prince's terror and despair.

"But a powerful sorceress found me and told me she would help me if I gave her some of my scales. Dragon scales are a rare and valuable commodity among magicians, apparently. She restored me to some semblance of a human shape, and gave me power over my dragon form.

"Once I had full control over my transformations and discovered all my hidden dragon powers, I sought to return home, to reunite with my father. But when I arrived at the palace, there was nothing but bones and ashes. Remnants of an old war.

"Once I discovered that your father was responsible, I began my campaign of vengeance against your tiny little kingdom." the dragon said, and gently tucked away a stray piece of the prince's golden hair behind his ear. Philip's jaw quivered as if fighting to unleash the words that were trapped inside his mouth.

"Do you wish to speak, my little pet?" Maleficent asked. And the prince nodded.

"Then speak," the dragon commanded.

"P-please, my father will make amends, I can ask him to... "

"Amends? What on earth could your father possibly do to bring back all my stolen years, undo all the harm he did to my people and my kingdom?" Maleficent asked, smiling lazily.

"B-but... " The prince said.

"No, I already have what your father loves most in the world," the dragon said. "And knowing that he will never again see it is the punishment I demand."

"W-what will you do to me?" the prince asked, wondering how much longer he had before he met his death.

"Oh, what indeed," the dragon said with a gleam in his eye.

"Please, don't hurt me," the prince begged.

"Oh, don't worry, my young prince, I won't kill you. No, no, you are much too precious for that, but I do have many unspeakable things in mind in store for you, and who knows you may even enjoy them," Maleficent said, laughing.

Maleficent lifted the prince to his feet as he stood up. He took Philip's hand and led him deeper into the skeleton of the castle, through several dark corridors, up a flight of stairs, to the highest room of the tallest tower, where he took his first taste of the prince.

And what a luxurious meal it was.

The prince could only lay helplessly as he was ravaged and violated by the dragon, unable to scream for help or mercy.

Devastated at the disappearance of his son, the king fell into deep despair, and as his hope crumbled, so did his kingdom. The prince now, a prisoner at Black Mountain, became the dragon's personal plaything, a helpless victim to his perverted games.

Prince Philip was kept young and alive by the dragon's magic, and as the years passed, the prince slowly began to delight in the delicious torture of his cruel master. An immortal slave, completely obedient to the whims and demands of the very monster he once swore to slay.

The dragon, satisfied with his vengeance upon the kingdom, showered his royal captive with merciless punishment and sweet affection.

This was going to be such fun, the dragon thought as he watched the prince perform his many unmentionable chores.

The memory of the missing prince soon became but a legend,

then, a forgotten dream; his name a mere whisper in the endless noise of history, now lost forever to the winds of time, never to be uttered again.

The Price of Magic

There once was an orphan girl named Ella, who once lived a life of comfort, grace, and wealth. However, not soon after her mother's death at the hands of a mysterious illness, Ella's father remarried, and brought into their crumbling home a cruel stranger and her two spiteful offspring.

Thus began Ella's tale of terror, for after her father's suspicious demise three weeks before her 13th birthday, her stepmother and two stepsisters revealed their true nature.

With no one left alive to protect her from their malice, Ella was forced to become a servant to the three wretched women, who were quite miserly with her father's wealth, even as they squandered it on luxurious gowns and expensive jewelry.

They spared no expenses on their adornments, but would not even pay a penny for a maid. Ella was to be the housekeeper, the cook, and whatever else they needed her to be, and they would often work her day and night till she was too tired to stand.

Ella would cry herself to sleep each night, praying for a miracle that would not come.

But one day, as she was cleaning the attic, Ella came upon her late mother's belongings, which she had never dared touch even as a young child.

Now, all the mysterious objects that were once forbidden to

her eyes lay unguarded, awaiting her discovery within the depths of an ancient chest. Seeing no reason to withhold her curiosity, Ella opened the lid to unearth the secrets that had eluded her all her life.

She was disappointed to see that the chest was mostly empty, save a few jars filled with herbs she did not recognize with names she had never heard of like "belladonna", "hemlock", "nightshade", and "wolfsbane". Many other objects littered the bottom, like a cat's skull, a chunk of amethyst and an intricately carved wooden staff.

In the middle of the clutter was a large leather-bound book studded with gems. She placed it on her lap and opened the cover. In the dim light of her lamp, she read the first words that greeted her, on the very first page, written in exquisite black ink.

A Grimoire for Novice Sorcerers

Ella flipped through several more pages before realizing what had fallen into her possession. It was a book of magic.

The strange herbs, the animal bones, the crystals, the wand. There was not a shadow of doubt in her mind.

Her mother was a witch.

But there was more. Ella noticed that one of the pages of the spellbook, the grimoire, was marked by a black ribbon. She turned to the marked page and read what was inscribed in the margin.

For my dear Ella, I pray you will never have need of this.

The page in question was a spell called "The Mandrake Root", and contained instructions on the making of a talisman. The main ingredient was the root of a mandragora plant, that, when prepared correctly, will grant all your wishes and give you a long and happy life.

"What nonsense," Ella thought, even as she entertained the idea of a magical root that could spell the end of all her troubles, something that her mother apparently thought she needed. Ella closed the book, and put it back in the chest, closing the lid as she did so.

"Ella! Where's my afternoon tea?!" screamed a rude voice down below.

"Coming mother!" Ella replied, and left the attic.

Her stepfamily was waiting downstairs for drinks and biscuits whilst excitedly discussing the royal ball, a grand occasion that was held in the fall for only three days in a year. However, it was still months away and her stepsisters were already considering their garment options. Ella listened to their entitled ravings as she prepared their refreshments.

"Oh, we shall have the most splendid gowns," Anastasia yelled, flashing her buck-toothed smile.

"No, I shall be wearing the most splendid gown," Drizella argued, raising her crooked nose arrogantly in the air.

"Nothing but the best for my two precious ones," said Lady Esmerelda, matriarch of the household and cruel conservator of the Tremaine fortune.

"Hurry up with those biscuits, you oaf," Esmerelda screamed at her stepdaughter.

"Yes, mother," Ella replied. Once she served them, she dared to ask.

"May I go to the ball?"

Her stepmother and stepsisters looked at her in disbelief, before breaking into laughter.

"The prince is looking for a wife, dear sister," Drizella explained as if to a child. "We'll be sure to send you an invitation if he is ever in need of a maid."

"Besides, you don't even have a dress," said Anastasia as she chomped on her biscuit. "And we're certainly not lending you any of ours."

"Go bother the rats with your daydreaming, child, and let us enjoy our food in peace," said Esmerelda with a dismissive wave of her hand.

Ella quietly excused herself from the kitchen. She had served these ugly, ungrateful hags for years. Many times she had thought of poisoning their tea, or smothering them in their sleep, but was stopped only by the image of the hangman's noose around her neck.

Even in the small town where she lived, unexplained deaths still rose suspicion and murder was still punishable by death.

Cold tears of sadness slowly turned into hot tears of rage. Then Ella remembered the book of magic.

Did she dare dabble in the dark arts as her mother did before her?

Ella had imagined all the ways she would escape from the wretched life she was dealt with, but never had the courage to do so. Perhaps magic was the answer.

That evening, after finishing her chores, Ella silently crept back into the attic to retrieve the grimoire and read its contents from front to back. She decided that there was no harm in performing a simple spell, especially if there was a small chance that it could work.

On a Monday night a few days after the spring equinox, when she was sure that everyone in the house was fast asleep, Ella stole away into the dead of night to harvest the ingredient that was so essential in the making of the talisman.

Fortunately for Ella, her mother had left detailed instructions on where to find a mandragora, almost as if she had attempted the spell before.

Her mother's notes led her to the middle of a cemetery, before the grave of a hanged man, and sure enough, there was a mandragora plant, which Ella was able to identify by the light of a single burning lamp.

She grasped the leaves firmly in one hand and chanted the words to an incantation: "By all the powers of heaven, and all the powers of hell, awaken my guardian spirit, by the words of this spell, fulfill my heart's desires, concealed from mortal's sight, in wakefulness and in sleep, in darkness and in light."

The moment Ella uprooted the plant, an unholy cry thundered from its strange, human-shaped root, as if it were a screaming infant. Ella quickly doused it in white wine as the book instructed, and the hellish shrieking stopped.

She then buried the root in the middle of a crossroads, and for thirty days she watered it with cow's milk mixed with three drops of her own blood before drying it in an oven heated with branches of verbena.

For the final preparation, Ella anointed it with abremalin oil and wrapped it in a silk scarf, to be hidden away until its powers were needed. That night before bed, Ella fed the root three drops of her blood, as was the price decreed by her mother's grimoire, and whispered silently to her little friend.

"I wish for good fortune and happiness," she said, hoping with all her heart that her efforts were not in vain.

***

On the day of the royal ball, much to her delight, Ella's stepmother and stepsisters had fallen violently ill from a cold. She left each of them some broth, a kindness they did not deserve, and left them in the throes of their malady.

They did not bother her for the rest of the day, which gave her plenty of time to prepare for the ball. Excited and full of hope, Ella unearthed one of her mother's old ball gowns, a splendid blue dress untouched by the ravages of time, and slipped into its delicate embrace.

She knocked on her stepmother's bedroom door before she left, relieved to hear nothing but silence, courtesy of the potent sleeping potion she brewed earlier. Her mother's grimoire was full of useful tricks.

Her luck did not end there. As Ella waited by the side of the road wondering how she would get to the palace, a carriage clomped by, and a kind couple offered her a ride, which she graciously accepted.

Ella dared not hope that a strange root was the source of all this fortuity, but it seemed that the magic was working its charm, even as it lay hidden underneath her pillow.

Ella met the prince for the first time that night, who found her to be the most enchanting of all the maidens who attended the ball that evening. They shared a brief dance before he spirited her away from the great ballroom, into the privacy of the royal garden, where they talked for what seemed like hours.

"I am quite enamored by you, Ms. Tremaine," Prince Eric said, as he kissed the back of Ella's hand.

"Likewise, my prince," she replied. Her heart was all aglow with golden bliss. "And please, call me Ella."

"Will I see you again, Ella?"

"Yes," Ella said, hoping that her good fortune will last for a few more days, if only to see the prince once more. She cared so very little for the hollow extravagance of the royal ball, not when her heart was now so smitten.

As the clock struck midnight, Ella reluctantly excused herself, much to the prince's disappointment. They exchanged a farewell kiss before she disappeared into the night.

Relieved to see neither her stepmother nor her stepsisters waiting for her at home with tools of punishment, she quietly slipped into her room, where she made one last wish to the mandrake root.

"I wish for the prince to be mine," and drifted into the most pleasant of dreams.

***

Ella dared to return to the ball for the next two nights, never forgetting to first attend to her stepfamily, whose affliction did not seem to be improving. Alongside the sleeping potion, they proved to be no more a threat than a shark with all its teeth removed.

On the second night, she was dismayed to find more girls present at the palace, each one more beautiful and enchanting than the next. The prince was speaking to one of them as Ella entered the ballroom.

To her surprise, he abandoned the conversation and made his way towards her, eyes full of deep, warm affection, as if he were witnessing the stars for the first time.

Prince Eric took Ella's hand and kissed it, before all those present. Ella suddenly found herself becoming the focus of a hundred envious stares.

"I am glad you could make it. Come, I would like you to meet my parents."

"The king and queen?" Ella asked nervously.

"Yes, but have no fear, I have told them only wonderful things about you."

Ella was led before the monarchs of the kingdom, the prince's hand in hers. She curtsied politely before the king and queen, and flashed her best smile. Unfortunately, they did not seem impressed when she told them her family name, which did not belong to any of the noble houses of the land.

"Forgive me," Prince Eric said to her when they were once again within the silent sanctuary of the royal garden. "My parents insisted I find myself a nobleman's daughter," he confessed, looking sadly into her eyes.

"Are you sure you wish to court me? I am after all a commoner and an orphan as well," Ella said. "Hardly the kind of girl who should marry a prince," she said, hoping he did not feel the same way.

"My heart desires what it desires, and I only have eyes for you,"

Prince Eric said. But Ella was not convinced. It seems there were still more obstacles standing in the way of the life she had always dreamed for herself.

She fed the mandrake once more when she returned home that night and made a third wish.

"I wish for the king and queen to accept me as their own with an open heart."

On the third and final night of the royal ball, the prince led Ella once more to their secret hiding place among the royal roses and knelt before her, a ring in hand.

"Isabella Marie Tremaine, will you do me the honor of being my wife?" said the prince.

"... but the king and queen... " Ella asked, surprised, wondering if she was still asleep, dreaming of another life in another world.

"My parents have given us their blessing," Eric explained.

"Are you sure, my prince? I am not a nobleman's daughter, or a princess. And I have no gold to speak of."

"Your company and love is the only gold I need," he said and slipped the diamond ring on Ella's finger. She felt as if the stone held a star deep within its heart.

Ella did not return home that night, but was offered a room in the palace, with a large bed lined with silken sheets, a handmaiden at her beck and call, and possibly even a magnificent breakfast waiting for her in the morning.

It seemed as though everything was falling into place perfectly thanks to the mandrake root, which Ella brought with her to the palace on the final night of the ball. She kissed it goodnight before burying herself within the embrace of her luxurious bedsheets and falling into peaceful slumber.

***

However, Ella's absence in the Tremaine household did not go unnoticed and sure enough, just as her stepmother and stepsisters recovered from their illness, they started to search for her, puzzled at her sudden disappearance.

They reassured themselves that the girl had finally run away, driven off to some faraway town never to return, leaving the Tremaine fortune entirely in their waiting hands.

It was not until months later, when the king issued a public invitation to the prince's wedding, that they found Ella. Not in the crowd of people who had gathered to witness the event, but standing at the bridal dais with the prince, their hands entwined, about to be united in holy matrimony.

"Ella? You wretched thing!" Esmerelda screamed as she cut her way through the sea of merry guests like a wrathful blade, with her two stepdaughters following close behind. The crowd fell silent as they approached the magnificent arch.

"What do you think you are doing? Forgive me Your Highness, this girl, she has tricked you, she is not worthy to be your wife, she is but a maid, an ungrateful orphan girl..."

Ella stared at them coldly, looking regal and otherworldly in her snow-white wedding gown, a sight truly to behold, and whispered in the prince's ear. He gestured with a hand and the royal guards were summoned.

They dragged the three hysterical women away, and the wedding procession continued as if nothing out of the ordinary had happened.

From the depths of the dungeons in which they were now imprisoned, Esmerelda, Drizella and Anastasia could do nothing but wrestle against their chains and scream for mercy, their cries drowned out by the cheerful noises of the celebration above.

***

As the years went by, Princess Ella settled happily into her new role as a member of the royal court and wife to the prince.

By day, she would escort her husband as he attended his many royal duties, rubbing shoulders with dignitaries and ambassadors to address the needs and worries of the kingdom. But by night she would hone her dark magics in secret, in a private chamber she had disguised as a reading room.

The mandrake root, as potent as ever, enhanced her power a hundredfold. Ella could now do things that she once thought were impossible; like walking into a person's dreams, looking into their thoughts, rewriting their memories and even bending their minds to her will.

She could make a flower blossom from a seed, or reduce it to ashes with a look. She could bring flames to life and extinguish them just as easily with a breath. She could kill with a touch and bring a soul on the brink of death back to the land of the living with but a single word.

But her most important magic, one she performed every full moon night without fail, was a spell to preserve her beauty and youth, so that even as the years ravaged all those around her, she would remain untouched by the cruel hands of Time.

But as her magic grew, so did the void in her heart, and soon Ella hungered for more. The innocent girl she once was, who allowed herself to be mistreated and disgraced for years, was dead. And in her place stood a vengeful goddess, ready to claim her rightful place in the world.

As fate would have it, ten years later, the king and queen tragically passed while on a voyage across the sea, leaving the kingdom in the prince's hands. Ella was crowned queen the day after the royal funeral, her black coronation gown a pretentious gesture of grief at the untimely demise of Eric's beloved parents.

Queen Ella ruled for years and years, her beauty and splendor unrivalled even by the fairest maidens in the land, whom she would curse with ugliness whenever any of them grew too beautiful for her liking.

No one was safe, for her reach was infinite, courtesy of a scrying mirror that would warn her anytime a young girl was close to surpassing her beauty.

With her heart eclipsed by a lust for power, Ella could no longer derive joy from her husband's affection, the man she had once loved more than life itself.

Trapped in a spell that kept his mind weary and confused, King Eric became but a subservient puppet, obedient to her will. Even under her invisible tyranny, the kingdom prospered, for the magic that preserved her youth, also bestowed great wisdom and insight, gifts she used to govern the land.

But Ella's dark reign was not to be.

***

One day a new maid, who had not been told to stay away from the forbidden reading room, discovered the Queen's sorcerous accoutrements, stowed away in an ornate wooden closet.

The young maid had opened it with the sole purpose of cleaning its contents, only to find the mandrake root, lying innocently in a golden box, just as the Queen herself entered the room.

Seeing her prized possession in the hands of another, Queen Ella exploded into wrathful hysterics. She seized the mandrake root from the young maid's hand.

"You foolish girl, what have you done?!" She screamed.

"Forgive me, Your Highness," the maid stammered.

"Who asked you to enter this room?!"

"I-I was not told, Your Highness, please forgive me," the young maid said close to tears.

"Leave my sight, you wretched little thing, I'll have your head for this!" Ella screamed once more just as the girl fled from the room in terror.

But the damage had been done. And Ella knew this.

The mandrake root was a powerful talisman that could give you all you ever desired, but at a cost. Should it be seen by anyone other than the person who created it, the talisman would lose its power, forever.

And every wish it has ever granted will be undone.

Ella could do nothing as the mandrake root shriveled in her hand, and withered away, leaving nothing but a pile of dust on the floor.

The queen's renowned and otherworldly beauty faded not long after that, along with whatever unnatural powers she attained throughout the years. The king, her husband, slowly grew weary of her presence in the palace, his love for her, that once burned as bright as the sun, now as gray as ash.

He conjured rumors of her infidelity as a ploy to exile her from the palace. Soon, Ella, stripped of her title and her crown, was banished from the royal court.

She returned to her former home, now a bitter old woman who once had everything she could ever want, but was tempted by the empty promise of beauty and power.

Ella spent the rest of her sunset years reliving her glory days and doing anything she can to regain what she lost, but no spell, potion or talisman she crafted could restore her magic, her youth or her happiness.

Decades into the future, long after Ella's death, the Tremaine manor fell into the hands of another family. Their youngest daughter, whom they named Grimhilda, found the previous owner's belongings, and among them, the fabled grimoire that started this tragic tale.

As the young girl turned the pages of the book, and read its cursed contents, the echo of something long forgotten began to awaken.

Deep within Grimhilda's soul, slumbering like a dragon, stirred the restless shadow of the old queen, patiently waiting for the moment it would reawaken within the body of this young vessel, to bring forth a new reign of darkness upon the land.

Acknowledgements

To my publisher and friend, Charissa Ong. Thank you for believing in me and giving me a second chance, even when the odds never seemed to be in my favor.

To my Muse, who works invisibly in the astral world to deliver me these incredible works of art. Whoever you are, you need a pay raise, bestie.

To my readers and followers who have loyally supported me throughout my harrowing career as a new author. Y'all are amazing.

Finally, to my family and friends. Thank you for staying oblivious and allowing me to create in peace.

About the Author

Born in the heart of Johor Bahru in the spring of 1994, Zack Shah is a city boy with a wild soul. A lover of the written word since childhood, Zack Shah first fell head over heels with fantasy fiction but later began a tumultuous and passionate love affair with poetry, a relationship that culminated in "More than Words", his debut publication and crowning achievement.

When he's not crafting poems or short stories, Zack likes to write opinion pieces on various topics on his blog, mainly entertainment, pop culture and social issues, depending on what's trending at the current time.

"A Strange and Wicked Magic" is his second book with Penwings Publishing. Follow Zack Shah on his Instagram: @zackshahpoet

About the Book

A dark but familiar sequel to the best-selling "More than Words", Zack Shah returns with a much-anticipated second volume of poetry and prose titled "A Strange and Wicked Magic".

Haunting, beautiful and provocative, this new collection unravels the ambivalent nature of love, how it is neither good nor bad but both: venom and nectar, poison and cure, heaven and hell.

This book will take you through the highs and lows of it all, the pain and the pleasure, the chaos and the calm, the hurting and the healing.

A bittersweet read for the lovelorn, the lonely and the lost.

Books by Penwings

MORE THAN WORDS
By Zack Shah

A diary, a love letter and a storybook all rolled into one, Zack Shah bares it all in his debut poetry collection. #MTW is a collection where each page is a small window into a world where reality and imagination are childhood friends. From the innocence of young romance to the dangers of desire, experience the entire spectrum of human emotion laced in between his crafted words.

QUESTIONS TO OUR ANSWERS
By Timothy Joshua

#QTOA is a poetry and fiction book containing three main chapters, centred around questions one would ask during different stages of a relationship: What are we? Where are we going? How are we getting there? The poems, juxtaposed with short stories, take readers on a deeply reflective journey as they contemplate the deepest thoughts and hopes they carry for their past and present relationships.

DAYLIGHT DIALOGUES
By Charissa Ong Ty

Back by popular demand, Charissa Ong Ty's second Poetry and Short Stories book, #DaylightDialogues, re-explores heartbreak, deep aspirations of love, self-actualization and fictional short stories.

Pushing her boundaries with more challenging technical poetry writing, she hopes her readership would appreciate Daylight Dialogues as much as they did Midnight Monologues.

MIDNIGHT MONOLOGUES
By Charissa Ong Ty

No.1 Best-Selling English Poetry and Short Stories is sold in major bookstores in Malaysia, Singapore and the Philippines. #MidnightMonologues is divided into four parts: LOST, FOUND, HOPE, and Short Stories. In an age of decreased readership and short attention spans, this book aims to ignite the readers' imagination; with short, melodious writing.

POETHREE O' CLOCK BOXSET

By Charissa Ong Ty

Charissa Ong released a special collectible box set that includes her best-selling titles, Midnight Monologues, Daylight Dialogues along with a new illustrated poetry book, 'What Does Your Name Mean?'. The new poetry book brings readers on a journey of self-identity and addresses the failures and darkness one faces in a safe light.

MIDNIGHT MONOLOGUES AUDIOBOOK

By Charissa Ong Ty

Midnight Monologues Audiobook has two renditions. A female reader and a male reader. Sit back and relax while we read these beautiful stories out to you as you are about to go to sleep, while you're on a slow drive home from work or on a balcony with hot Camomile tea on a breezy, Saturday afternoon.

These audiobooks are available on our website as well as on international audiobook platforms.

www.ingramcontent.com/pod-product-compliance
Lightning Source LLC
La Vergne TN
LVHW091158150826
845672LV00005B/1187

* 9 7 8 9 6 7 1 4 2 2 7 7 9 *